MRS. MUDGIE AND MR. JAMES

Mrs. Mudgie and Mr. James

by JUDITH HOLLANDS
illustrated by MOLLY DELANEY

ATHENEUM   1988   NEW YORK

For my mother and father—J.H.

To my parents—M.D.

Atheneum, Macmillan Publishing Company, 866 Third Avenue, New York, NY 10022
Collier Macmillan Canada, Inc.
First Edition   Printed in Japan   10 9 8 7 6 5 4 3 2 1

Library of Congress Cataloging-in-Publication Data
Hollands, Judith Winship.   Mrs. Mudgie and Mr. James.
Summary: Tabitha and Timothy compare the characteristics of their imaginary friends.
[1. Imaginary playmates—Fiction]   I. Delaney, Molly, ill.   II. Title.
PZ7.H724714Mr   1988   [E]   87-35143   ISBN 0-689-31389-6

"Don't sit there!" Tabitha hollered. "That's Mrs. Mudgie's place!"

Timothy jumped up and looked all around. "But I don't see anyone," he said.

"That's because she's imaginary," said Tabitha in her smarty voice. "I made her up in my mind and she's my best friend."

Timothy just stood there. It wasn't fair. Mrs. Mudgie
got tea and black jelly beans and she wasn't even real.
"Well, I have an imaginary friend too," said Timothy.
"I made him up in my mind and his name is Mr. James."

Tabitha folded her arms and looked straight at Timothy. "What's he like?" she asked.

Timothy thought for a minute. "What is Mrs. Mudgie like?"

"Oh, she's a tiny little lady," said Tabitha. "She always wears a floppy hat with bows, purple tulips, and lots of feathers. She's a very interesting person."

"Well," Timothy said, "Mr. James is tall and has a long red mustache that nobody makes him cut. He has a plaid vest with shiny buttons and a tall black hat."

Tabitha sniffed. "A tall black hat? That sounds sort of plain and ordinary."

"Well, not really," said Timothy, "because when Mr. James takes his hat off, he can pull all kinds of things out of it. Just like a magic hat. Mr. James is probably magic all over too."

"Well, Mrs. Mudgie makes flags for a living," Tabitha said. "She makes all the flags for countries and parades and girl scout troops, and she does it all by herself. She doesn't need magic because she has quick little fingers."

"Mr. James has quick fingers too. He's an artist. He paints murals on the sides of tall buildings—all in one day. And at Christmas time, he paints designs on Christmas tree balls, and he even paints red and green stripes on his hat to make it look Christmasy too."

"Red and green stripes?" said Tabitha. "That might be interesting."

"But Mrs. Mudgie has lots of talent. She can sing operas. She can break all the crystal doodads on a fancy chandelier when she hits her highest note."

"Mr. James can play cymbals and a drum and a harmonica all at the same time," said Timothy. "He's a one-man band. And, with his free hand, he juggles colored popcorn balls."

"Well, Mrs. Mudgie has taps on her high-heeled shoes and she can do shuffle-hop-steps while she whistles 'Yankee Doodle Dandy' and drinks a glass of water."

"Wait a minute," Timothy said. "That's impossible."

"Mrs. Mudgie can do anything," Tabitha said. "She's a very interesting person."

"Well, Mr. James can yodel. And when Mr. James yodels, all the sheep in the countryside come running."

"Mrs. Mudgie is allergic to sheep."
"Oh," Timothy said. "That's too bad."

"But Mrs. Mudgie has lots and lots of toy animals. They don't bother her allergies. She has practically every animal in the world. And every time she has a birthday or it's Valentine's Day or even Wednesday, she gets another one wrapped up in a big box."

"Well, Mr. James has every toy car ever made. He even has a Bugatti big enough to ride around in. He has so many toys he has to have a special trailer behind the Bugatti to hold them all."

"Mrs. Mudgie's dog Rupert would really like that. He's part sheepdog and part Airedale and he'd chase the wheels and bark like crazy."

"Well, Mr. James has an attack robot. And everywhere he goes, the robot makes sure nobody hurts him or his toys."

"Mrs. Mudgie would never let Rupert fight. Mrs. Mudgie takes care of her own problems. She used to be a strong lady in the circus and she has huge muscles. When she gets mad, people know she means business."

"When Mr. James puts on his monster mask
—the one with the rubber cheeks and the bulgy
eyebrows and the long yellow teeth—everybody
in the whole *world* gets scared and runs away."

Tabitha sniffed. "It's not nice to pick on
people who are smaller than yourself.
Mrs. Mudgie has *good* manners."

EXTREME
CAUTION!

"Mr. James was just kidding. He really has good manners too, when he tries. He says 'Thank you very much' and 'You're so very welcome.' He even likes to comb his hair and brush his teeth. He takes a bath every day, without being asked, and he uses a fancy brush to scrub his back extra clean."

"He sounds sort of interesting," said Tabitha. "Does Mr. James like tea?"

"Only with lots of sugar and served upside down," said Timothy.

"Mrs. Mudgie can do that. Uh-oh. But if she's not careful her hat will get all ruined."

"That's OK. Mr. James will give her his. He really has good manners."

"Well, Mrs. Mudgie has to go now. She has to take Rupert to the pet parlor. He's having his toenails clipped."

"Can Mr. James come too?" Timothy asked.

"Only if he leaves that awful robot behind."

"Who...him? He's only a toy. Mr. James will put him back in his trailer. And guess what? Mr. James has something for Mrs. Mudgie. He's found some leftover Christmas balls."

"Oh! Mrs. Mudgie will put them on her new hat. That was very thoughtful."

"Do you like tea?" Tabitha asked Timothy.

"Only with lots of black jelly beans," Timothy answered.

"How interesting," said Tabitha. She filled a little cup with tea and carefully picked nine black jelly beans out of her bag.

"Thank you very much," said Timothy.

"You're so very welcome," said Tabitha.